A Baby for Max

A Baby for Max

Text by Kathryn Lasky in the words of
Maxwell B. Knight

Photographs by Christopher G. Knight

Charles Scribner's Sons *New York*

Text copyright © 1984 Kathryn Lasky
Photographs copyright © 1984 Christopher G. Knight

Library of Congress Cataloging in Publication Data
Lasky, Kathryn   A baby for Max.
    Summary: Text and photographs record a five-year-old
as he awaits the birth of the family's new baby and
enjoys her afterward.
    1. Pregnancy—Juvenile literature. 2. Childbirth—
Juvenile literature. [1. Babies. 2 Brothers and
sisters] I. Knight, Maxwell B. II. Knight,
Christopher G., ill. III. Title.
RG525.5.L37   1984   306.8'75   84-5307
ISBN 0-684-18064-2

1 3 5 7 9 11 13 15 17 19   Q/C   20 18 16 14 12 10 8 6 4 2

Printed in the United States of America

To my baby sister
—*Max*

I'm Max Knight, and I'm having a baby. It's in Mom's tummy. It's the biggest tummy in the world. It's bigger than anybody else's.

Dad helped make the baby. It floats around in Mom's stomach, sometimes right side up, sometimes upside down, sometimes sideways.

I'm telling the baby, "Ena." That means "I love you."

I talk into Mom's belly button. The baby thinks there's a strange person out there talking to it. The baby doesn't know anything about outside.

Sometimes I pretend my Teddy is a baby.

I want the baby to be a boy, the same as me, but not the same size.

Mom and Dad want to call it Jacob if it's a boy. I don't want to call it Jacob. That's a chubby name. I'd like to call it Junior. Even if it is a girl.

My clothes are bigger than the baby's because I'm bigger. I used to be a baby when I wore these little clothes.

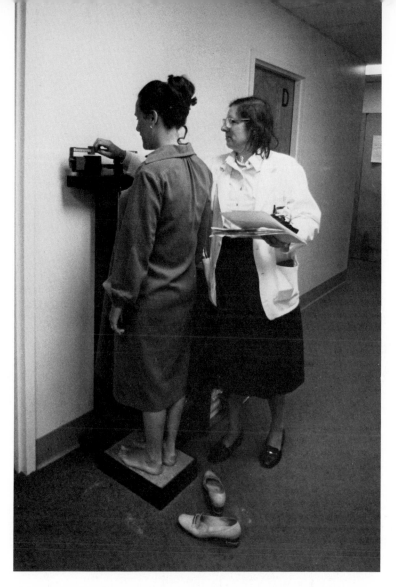

Mom has to go to the doctor who helps when the baby comes
out. I'm listening to the baby's heartbeat. It sounds like
ocean water washing, and somebody hammering, and fish
splashing.

I like the baby. I felt it kicking.
It kicks because it wants to get
out.

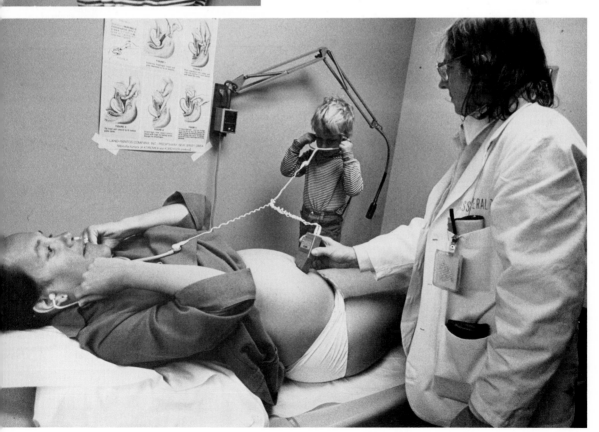

I visited the hospital where Mom will go to have the baby. When you're not used to it, the hospital is a little scary. They will put her in an electric bed that goes up and down. If she wants breakfast, they'll bring it on a tray.

They showed me how to diaper a doll. It wasn't too easy, but I did it. I first had to pull up the little sack the doll baby was in, then wipe its bottom so it wouldn't be dirty. I had to rub on Vaseline so it wouldn't be sore. Then I had to put it down on the diaper. I taped the diaper up, and that's how I diapered it.

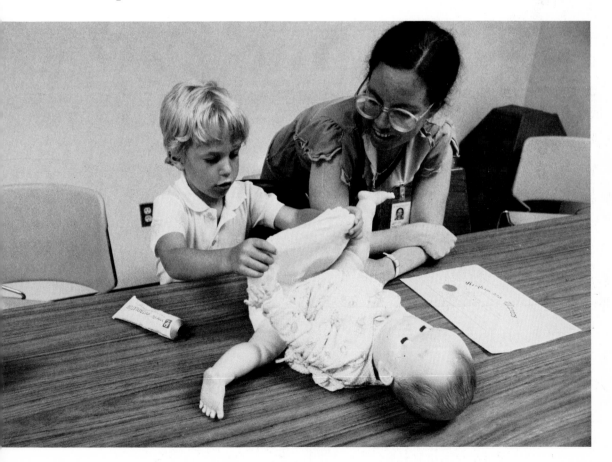

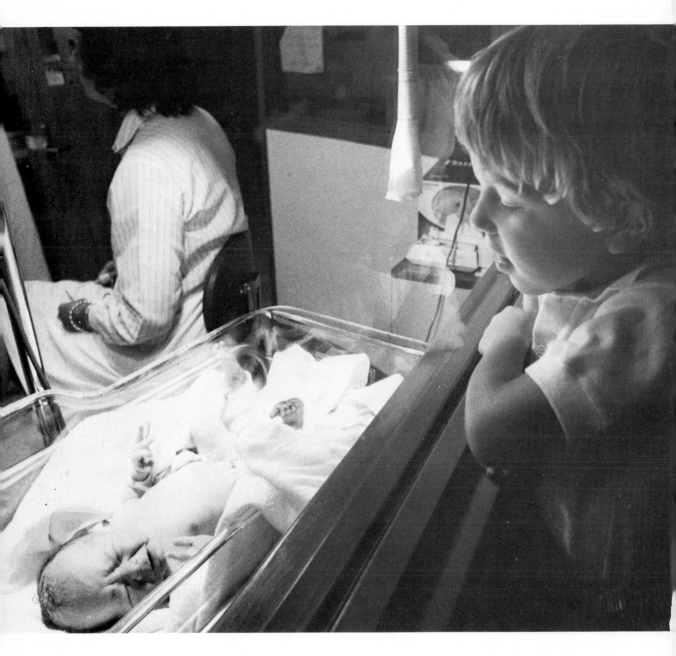

We looked at someone else's baby. It was crying a little.
Maybe it thought people were strange creatures.

When the baby squeals you try giving it food, and if it still squeals, you try a toy. If it plays with the toy, that's what it wanted.

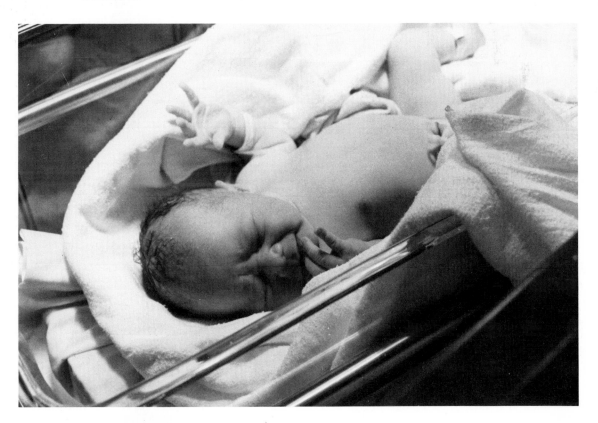

Mom moved my clothes from the big dresser to make room for the baby's clothes, but I want the big dresser because my clothes are already in it. Why don't we put the baby's clothes in the bottom drawer?

Mom showed me a sack you zip the baby into. I said, "Maybe we could zip it into that and sell it!"

Mom has been very tired lately. She wishes the baby would come out. I say, "Mom, would you just sit down, comfort yourself, and read me a story?" I help her by setting the table.

Dad and I made a changing table for the baby. I cut the
material to cover it and helped to staple it on. I'm good at
making things. I made the Empire State Building out of
blocks.

Mom said again how she wished the baby would come. I said she should do some exercises with me, and that would get it to come out.

I think it worked. That night, after I was asleep, Mom and Dad went to the hospital. Our friend Joyce came to stay with me.

When I woke up the next morning, Dad was already back to tell me what had happened. He was very happy. He told me I had a baby sister. Her name is Meribah. I said, "I had my baby. I thought it was going to come today. I'm a big brother." I felt happy.

I called my grandmother and grandfather to tell them we just had a new baby sister. I told them she is just what I wanted. I made some cards to take to the hospital. The one for Meribah says, "Meribah Grace, new baby, I love you." The other is for Mom. It says, "I love you," too.

At lunch time, all of a sudden I feel sad. Too many exciting things are happening, and it doesn't feel so nice. A baby-sitter is there and Mommy has gone away. I don't want the baby-sitter. Dad says he will take me to see Mom and Meribah at the hospital this afternoon.

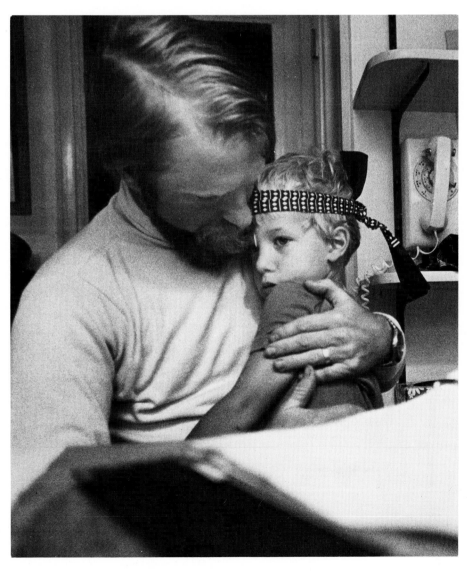

When we get to the hospital, I start running. We find
Mom's room. She is in bed with Meribah. Meribah is so
little! I like her little hands. She is nursing from Mom's
breast. Mom says, "Can you believe that our baby finally
came?"

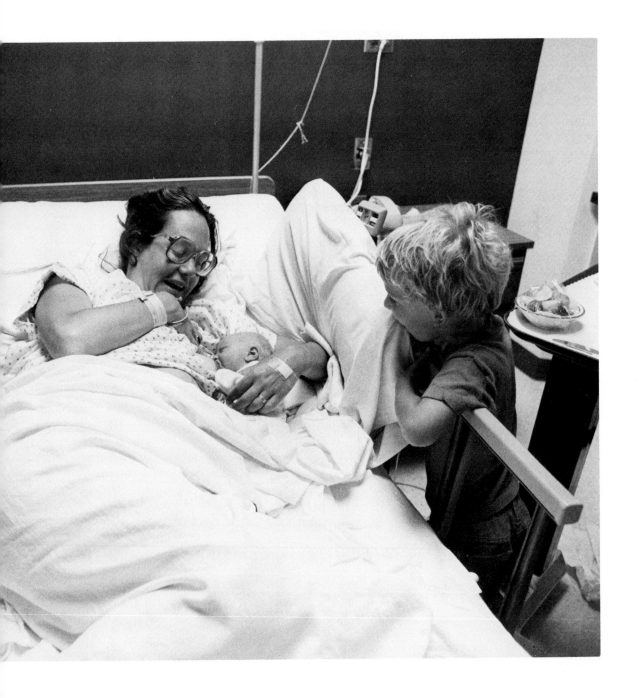

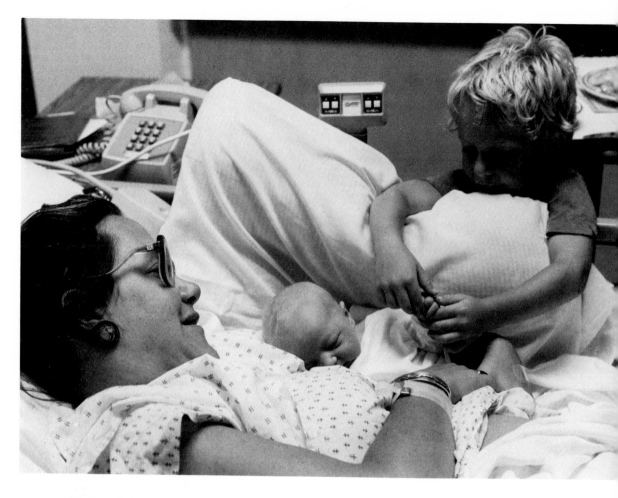

I give Mom the cards for her and Meribah. I like touching
Meribah. She is as soft as a lobster's skin after you take off
the shell. She doesn't know anything about the world. She
thinks this room is the world and there are only three people
in it.

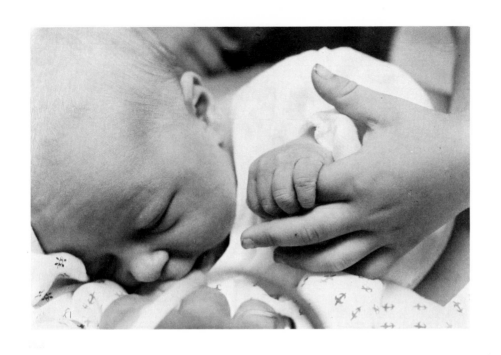

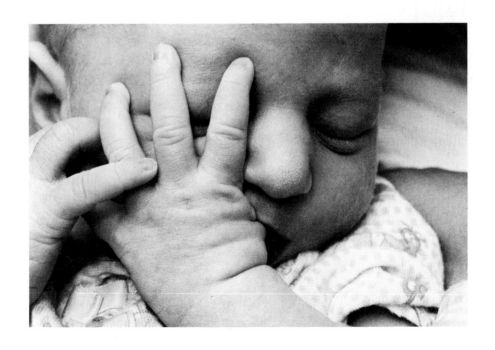

I dreamed last night that she had grown to be a big girl and
that we were playing together. Now she just likes sucking on
my finger.

Some days I feel angry because everybody's talking all the time about Meribah. Mom and Dad are always doing things with her like feeding her or changing her diaper. People are not paying enough attention to me.

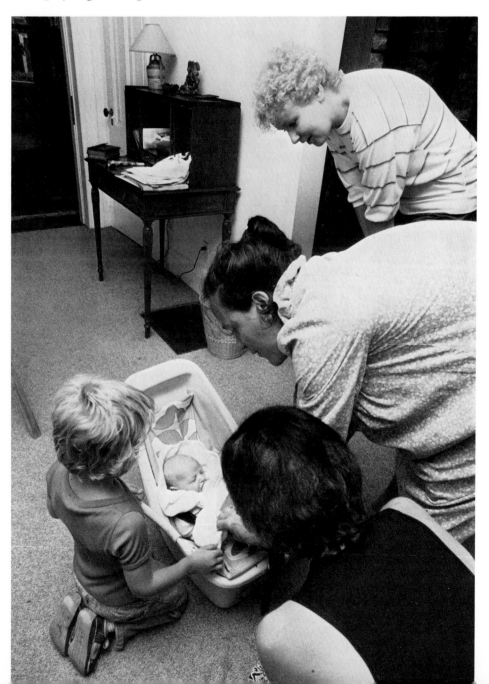

One day I was mad at Dad. I said I was so mad at him that I was going to take away all his clothes and send him to someplace where it's very cold, like South America.

I'm running away. I'm taking real food with me. I crawled under the dining table, and when Mom asked where I was, I said I was calling from New York.

Babies *are* nice, though. You have to be very gentle with them. Be very careful of their heads, feed them milk from a mother. Give a baby sister flowers or ferns or something beautiful like that.

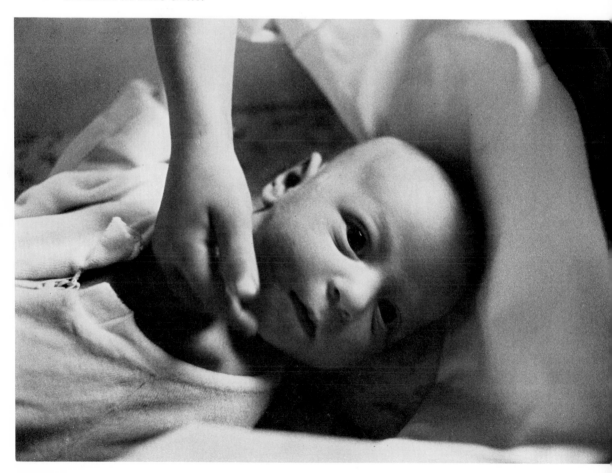

I made up a song for Meribah:

> Oh little baby, I love you
> When you crawl on your face so flat.
> When you sleep with your pacifier in your mouth
> I love you both north and south.

Mom showed me some pictures of when I was the same age as
Meribah is now. When I was a little baby, we didn't have to
pay attention to anyone else. There was just Dad, me, and
Mom.

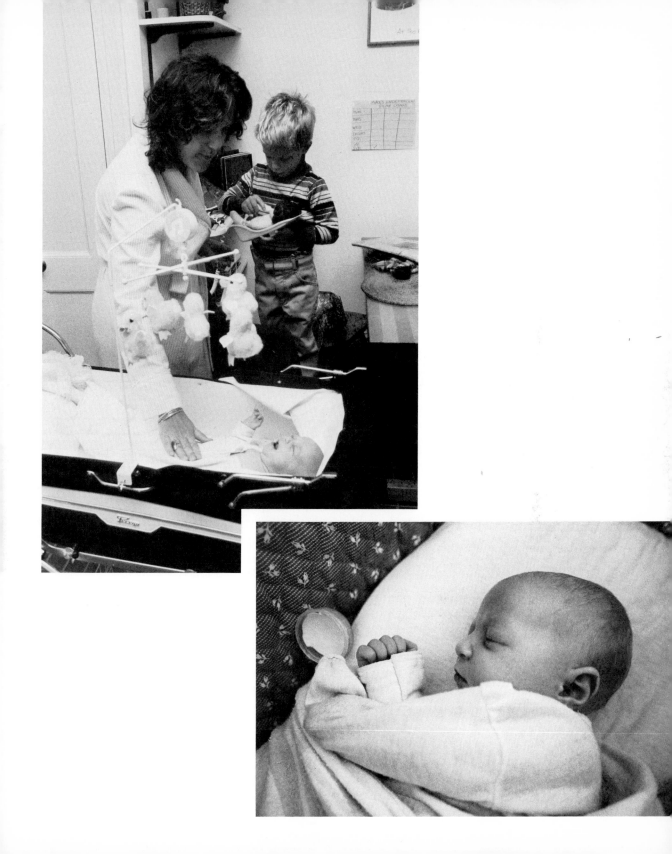

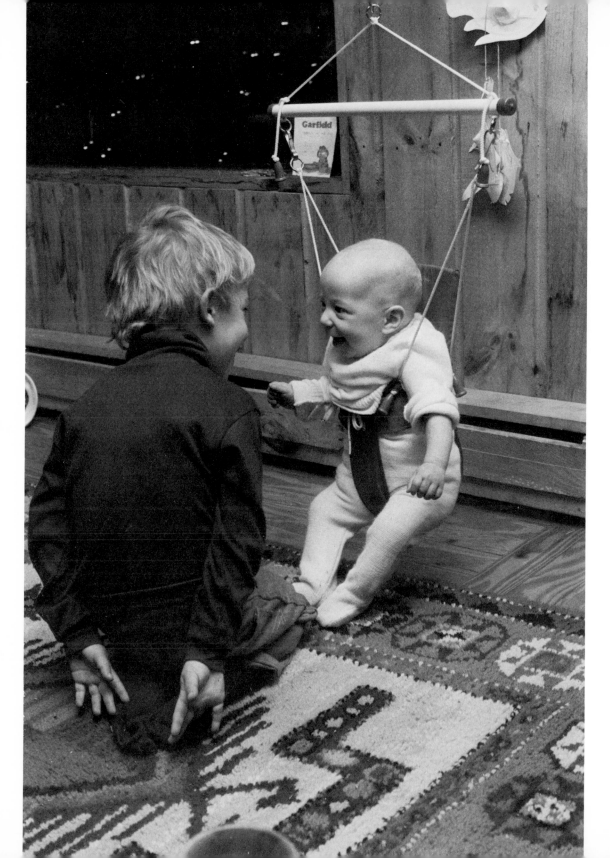

Still, I'm one of the luckiest people. Some people don't have any baby. Some people just have cats or dogs, but I'll have a baby for a pet. I'll play with the baby, so I won't have to play with Mom and Dad all the time. That will be nice, especially when they are busy.

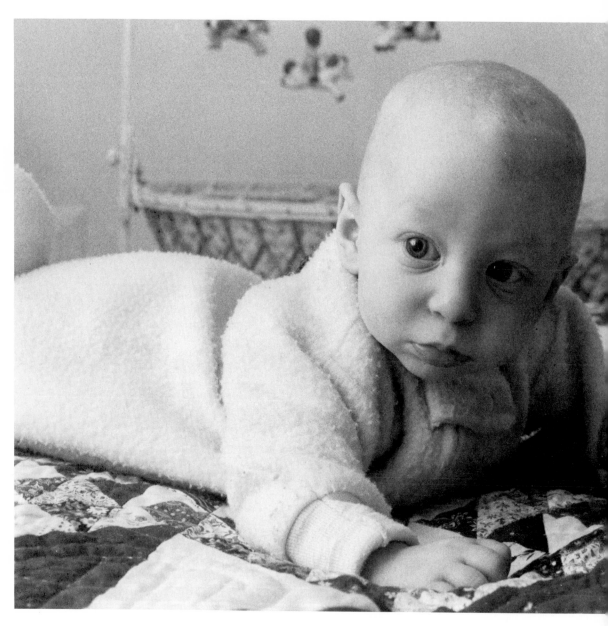

When she gets to be a toddler, we'll call her Bah. When she grows up to be a big girl, we'll call her Marie.

Now I call her Beba. Mom and
Dad started calling her that, too.

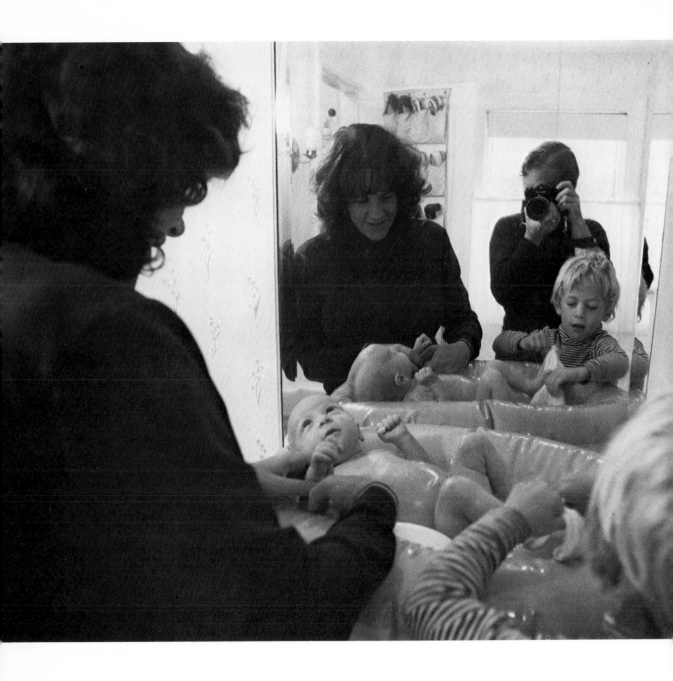

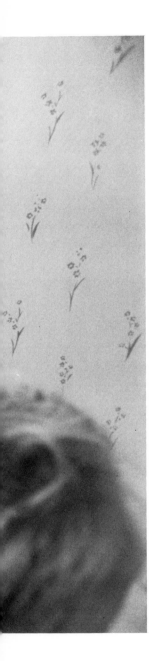

I like helping to give her a bath. She kicks
and splashes and makes a mess. I'm not
supposed to do that. She looks funny when
Mom dries her with the towel.

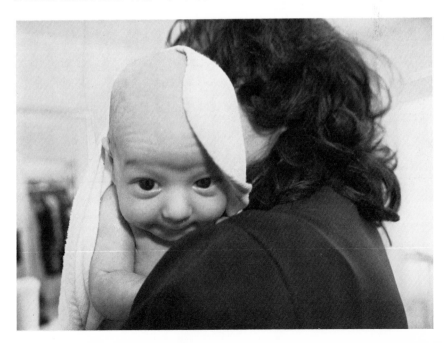

She can't play with me yet, but she has just learned how to smile. Mom says she won't learn how to walk till next year.

I'm almost five years old now, and I can even do gymnastics. I go to a class after school.

I'll always be older than she is, even when she grows up.

I just love babies. I love ours the most.